THE
WITCH'S
SPOON

by Mary Cunningham

illustrations by Marilyn Miller

Xerox Education Publications

XEROX

To Beth, with love

Text copyright © 1975 by Mary Cunningham Pierce
Illustrations copyright © 1975 by Xerox Corporation

Publishing, Executive, and Editorial Offices:
Xerox Education Publications
Middletown, Connecticut 06457

Library of Congress Catalogue Card Number: 74–22653
ISBN 0–88375–208–5

Weekly Reader Children's Book Club Edition
XEROX® is a trademark of Xerox Corporation.

There was something new in Grandma's curio cabinet. On the first day of their arrival to spend a week with Grandma, Tom and Lauren swarmed through her seaside cottage in a burst of high spirits. They banged their suitcases down on the old brick floor. They touched all the familiar furniture. They bounced on the bunk beds lined up on the sleeping porch. They smelled the special smell of the cottage, which was part pine forest and part the good salty sea smell.

Grandma had given them each a welcoming kiss and hug when their father had left them and driven away. And then she let them explore all the familiar nooks and crannies of the cottage.

It was Lauren who discovered the addition to the curio cabinet. It was on the lower shelf with the pearl-handled pistol and the lace bride's cap. "What's this big long spoon?" she asked. "It's new."

Tom came to join Lauren. "It's the first time there's ever been anything new in the curio cabinet," he exclaimed in amazement.

"It's not new," Grandma explained. "In fact, it's probably the oldest thing in the cabinet. But it's new to me. It's a witch's spoon."

"A witch's spoon!" the children chorused, eyes wide.

"Your Great-aunt Hannah left it to me in her will."

"She's the one who lived somewhere in Massachusetts," Tom recalled.

Grandma said, "She's not living now. But this witch's spoon has been a relic in the family from the time of the old witches' trials in Salem, Massachusetts, when witches were thought to be as much a problem to people as air pollution is now." Grandma's round face crinkled in a smile.

"Do you really believe a witch could have used this spoon?" Lauren asked.

"Witches, those I've seen in pictures," Tom said, "stirred their big old cauldrons with a stick." He was anxious to get into his swim trunks and out on the beach. He was already kicking off his shoes.

"There were, so they say, good witches and bad witches," Grandma informed them. "A spoon was used by good witches to stir love potions."

"Oh, mush and slush," Tom scoffed. "Who believes in that?"

"I do—I think," Lauren said a little uncertainly. "At least it's nice to think about love potions. I never heard of a witch's spoon before."

"They're very rare," Grandma conceded. "This is the only one I've ever seen." She opened the cabinet and let Lauren hold the spoon. This was a rule. If anyone wanted to touch anything in the cabinet, it had to be opened by Grandma.

The minute Lauren held the brightly polished silver spoon, which was larger than a tablespoon but not as large as a mixing spoon, she felt something odd. A delightful shiver of excitement went down her spine. "It's really magic," she whispered in awe. "I feel all goose pimply like something wonderful or different is going to happen."

Tom rolled his eyes. "You know Lauren and her imagination," he remarked to Grandma.

Grandma took the spoon away from Lauren and replaced it in the cabinet. "Imagination is very useful. It perks up the dullest moments if we let it."

"Well, I sure don't believe in witch's spoons, or witch's broomsticks, or pointed hats or witch's anything," Tom declared.

"But I did feel something different," Lauren insisted.

"That's because your week here *is* going to be different," Grandma told them. She sat in the rocking chair.

"What do you mean it's going to be different?" Tom asked.

Grandma picked up some sewing from a nearby table. "First of all, since you are old enough now to use judgment, you should have a June Day."

"But this is June. Aren't all our days June days?" Lauren questioned.

"A June Day is a special day when all the usual rules are cancelled. Long ago my own grandma gave me a June Day when I was allowed to do just as I wanted." Grandma sounded dreamy as she spoke again. "I've never forgotten it."

"What did you do?" both children asked.

"I'll tell you sometime," Grandma promised. Then she continued, "When your father and his brother were about your age, I gave them a June Day. And now it's your turn."

"Is it today?" Tom wanted to know.

"No," Grandma replied. "A June Day must be planned and looked forward to. Since this is Monday, I think Wednesday would be just right."

Lauren sat on the floor at Grandma's feet. "Tell us just how it will be."

"I'll cook breakfast at eight, lunch at twelve and supper at five, as usual, but if you are not here, that's all right. Any food not eaten at those times will be given to Mr. Bunby. He's not fond of cooking for himself anymore." Mr. Bunby was Grandma's neighbor and the children's friend.

"That's neat," Tom commented, thinking about how

4

frequently he'd had to interrupt some pleasant pastime to get back to meals.

"If you want to spend the day in the woods turtle hunting, try it. If your heart's desire is to explore the old Indian trail on the bluff top, you may."

Tom thought Grandma's idea of wanting to spend a whole day turtle hunting was pretty far out. He hadn't wanted to do that since he was a little kid of six. Exploring the old Indian trail was not exciting anymore either. He'd done that over and over. But the word "explore" pressed a button of daring in his mind. He knew exactly what he *did* want to explore.

"This should be a day you will always remember," Grandma was going on, "but there are two things to keep in mind."

"What are they?" Tom questioned.

Grandma adjusted her spectacles to thread her needle. "You have to remember that every box has its pill."

"Pill?" Lauren could not believe her ears. This talk of pills didn't sound like Grandma at all. Could the witch's spoon have cast some kind of spell over her?

"If you open the box and find a bitter pill, you have to swallow it," Grandma admonished. "That's what my own grandma told me."

"But all boxes don't have pills," Lauren rushed in. "Christmas and birthday present boxes don't have pills."

"That's because those gifts were chosen by people who love you or want to give you something nice, and they put them in pretty boxes. But what I'm referring to is all the other boxes of life that contain things you won't like."

Lauren reached back in memory to a story their teacher had read them in school. "You mean like Pandora's box, I guess."

Grandma nodded. "That's a good example. Pandora was so full of curiosity that she opened a box full of dreadful things, and Pandora had to suffer for it. So though the box you wish to open may seem to hold the most teasing of mysteries, consider carefully before you lift the lid. If there's a nip of danger in what you want to do, use your head before you start. In other words, I'm trusting you to use judgment. Before you go out for the day, you must write your general location on the kitchen blackboard where I keep the grocery list. You can just say, 'gone to town,' or 'gone to the beach,' or 'to the woods.'"

Tom grinned. "So if we aren't back by dark you can send bloodhounds after us."

"Yes," Grandma agreed, "you *must* be back by dark."

Tom did not say so aloud, but his plan probably would have a nip of danger. But he certainly knew enough to make it only a nip.

Lauren hadn't decided yet what her June Day adventure was going to be, so she just said, "Trust us, Grandma." On impulse she threw her arms around Grandma in a reassuring hug.

Grandma hugged back, saying, "I'm glad to hear that. If anything serious happens to you, I will get into trouble.

Your parents may not allow you to return here next summer."

"Gee, we won't do anything wild," Tom promised. "We're just going to have fun." His last words came from the sleeping porch, where he had dumped everything out of his suitcase. In another couple of minutes he had skinned out of his clothes and returned ready for the beach in tan swim trunks.

"Wait for me," Lauren called, almost as fast as Tom in getting into her bathing suit.

"There's one more thing that will be different about your vacation," Grandma told them. "But since you are so impatient to get to the beach, I'll tell you later."

"Oh, we're not that impatient—really we're not," Lauren insisted, her curiosity stirred.

Grandma gave her a loving spank. "Go along. "You'll hear the rest later."

"O.K.," Tom replied.

And since Tom really did seem to be hopping with impatience, Lauren scampered after him.

"Poison on the stones," Lauren called to her brother as they left the cottage.

"Poison on the stones," Tom responded, meaning that to walk on the stepping stones that led through Grandma's small garden was forbidden for the day and would bring bad luck.

Lauren was stuffing her bright blond hair into a swim cap as they ran, and her toe caught on a stepping stone and she fell. "Bad luck," she conceded cheerfully, but of course she didn't really believe it.

Tom waited while she rubbed her skinned knee, and then they were off at a clip, past Mr. Bunby's cottage next to Grandma's, then to the top of the bluff where a clearing in the grove of pines gave them their first entranced view of the water below. The breakers foamed and dashed on the white sandy beach, an inviting sight to city children.

There were winding wooden stairs, over a hundred of them, that took them down, down the bluff to the sea shore. There were two cozy resting places where the stairs widened to hold a bench. Over the years the children had given names to the two resting places.

On the first landing they had once found almost a dollar in change that had apparently slipped through a hole in someone's pocket. So this was called the money spot. "See any money?" Tom asked.

"No money today," Lauren replied. They always asked the question, even though there had been only that one time they found any.

"Here's the owl tree!" Tom yelled at the second landing, and he quickly climbed over the railing of the stairs to find a stout stick. He knocked it against the trunk of an old tree, split and hollow, where every year there had been a new baby owl in its nest high above them.

"There's a baby owl," Lauren called excitedly as a tiny fuzzy head appeared in the opening in response to the thud of the stick against the tree. "Oh, it's darling."

"Darling!" Tom mocked. "It's just a baby owl." It was part of the game to see the new owlet each year.

Breathless and happy, Lauren and Tom ran across the sand dunes to the water's edge. The blue sea before them, the swooping gulls, the sandpipers that strutted among the washed-up kelp were just as they remembered.

"Last one in the water is stinky Slinky, the black-footed ferret!" Tom yelled.

Lauren didn't mind being Slinky, the black-footed ferret. She loved all animals. Last summer a tiny ferret had come in from the woods and become lost in Grandma's tool shed. At Lauren's coaxing Mr. Bunby had made a wire cage, and the children had kept the little animal as a pet. Lauren had loved his slinky furry form, his bright eyes, and it had been hard to set him free in the woods when they left Grandma's.

"O.K., so I'm Slinky." She couldn't call her pet stinky. That was just Tom's way.

"You sure are," Tom agreed. Lauren waded knee deep in the cold water. Suddenly an impish grin appeared on Tom's face. He put a hand on her head, pushing her down gurgling and gasping into the icy water. Then she was bobbing up with a whoosh of relief, glad the plunge was over and a little mad at Tom's trick.

Tom's brown eyes were drawn in fascination to the spectacular pile of rocks that rose out of the water at one point and made a castle-like barrier along the shore. Tom and Lauren had clambered over the great rocks many

10

times, searching for shells and tiny sea creatures that lived in pools left by the dashing waves. But they had never, never explored the forbidden cave behind the mammoth rocks.

It was said that if you went far enough into the cave you would find a three-story cavern room with marvelous echoes and a group of rocky figures that looked like stone elephants. It was even said that under one of the fantastic elephants there was buried pirate's treasure.

Tom did not want Lauren to suspect that he was planning to explore the cave. He was not going far, of course. But he didn't want Lauren along. She might be frightened right away and want to turn back and spoil his adventure.

Tom and Lauren swam and played in the water until more and more people came to enjoy the beach. Tom was glad when at last Lauren was tired.

"I'm going to flop on a sand dune and bake," Lauren said. She stretched out, breathing in the smell of wild grasses in the dunes. The long, early morning ride with their father, who had brought them to Grandma's from the city, the play time in the water, and the lapping sounds of surf made her sleepy. On one last glance down the beach she saw Tom climbing over a pile of driftwood to the castle rocks.

After a while I'll go with him to hunt for shells, she thought. Her favorite shells were called angel's toenails. She loved the name, but they were hard to find. One minute she was thinking about her shell collection and the next she was sound asleep.

Tom looked back to his sleeping sister on the sand, happy she wasn't tagging along. He wanted a good look at the entrance to the cave alone.

Part of the way Tom had to go on his hands and knees. At high tide in rough weather the exploding waves polished the rocks and made them slick. Where they weren't slick there were jagged crusts of barnacles and slippery eel grass that made progress difficult.

Tom paused for breath. An unexpected sand dollar stamped with its five-pointed star caught his eye. There were some limpets and ghost fish in the little rock pools, too. But today he was more interested in getting to the high pinnacle of rock that shielded the entrance to the cave.

He lay as flat as he could on the rocky point and gazed down to the ledge of rock that hid the opening in the cliff side below. How had the pirates who'd hidden their treasure there ever found this opening? he wondered. Maybe the Indians knew about it and the pirates found out from them.

Remembering tales he'd heard from Mr. Bunby, he knew you had to snake your way in through the narrow opening. Then you came to a series of rooms. The last room was the one that held the rocky, elephant-like figures.

He would need a strong rope to loop over the pinnacle of the rock. He could let himself down hand under hand on that, the ten or twelve feet that would put him right at the mouth of the cave. Then he'd need a flashlight. That

would be easy. He knew Grandma had one in a kitchen cupboard for emergencies. He would take a sack just in case there was anything in the cave he wanted to bring back.

"Gee, I really am an explorer," he said aloud. As his plans unfolded, he thought about food to take along. A sandwich or two and a bottle of pop.

Back at the beach, Lauren woke to see clouds, bright crimson with sunset. She looked for Tom, but she couldn't see him. Suddenly she sat up straight. A strange sensation came over her. It was almost the same feeling she'd had when she held the witch's spoon from Grandma's curio cabinet.

She knew now what she wanted to do on her June Day. It would be her own secret adventure. Bounding along on a wave of excitement, she ran across the sand dunes to the long flight of stairs that led up the bluff side through the wind-twisted pines.

As Tom had done on their way down, she tapped with a stick on the trunk of the tree they called the owl tree. A moment later a little fuzzy owl head appeared at the hole. Two dark-tipped tufts stood up on the tiny head. Baby owl eyes blinked in the fading daylight.

Each year Lauren had longed to hold a baby owl. Looking at one now, she thought it would be nicer than anything she could imagine to cuddle and pet that tiny, fuzzy creature.

Then to her utter astonishment she saw another tiny head appear beside the first owlet. "Two baby owls!"

Lauren gasped. "There's never been two before. Oh, you sweet little things," she crooned, looking up.

Lauren, who loved reading everything about animals and birds, remembered that owls had the softest feathers of any bird. They made it possible for them to fly silently and swoop down on their prey. So a baby owl must be the most downy baby in the world.

Lauren stood on the bench and stretched up. But the owl's home was still out of reach. She was taller and stronger this year. She looked at the branches of the tree, and she was sure she could climb. She would hold a baby owl, maybe both of them.

Noises from the foot of the stairs told her other beachers were about to start up. So she quickly jumped down from the bench and climbed the stairs.

The best plan was to come out early on her June Day before people wanted to go to the beach. She'd have to get away from Tom, who would certainly think her silly to want to hold a baby owl. But it was her heart's desire, so she could be as silly as she liked. She couldn't really understand her longing herself. It wasn't like dying to go to a party or waiting all pins and needles for Christmas or Halloween.

Tom had already returned to the cottage, and Grandma was putting a heaping plate of sweet corn on the table, along with cold ham, muffins and other good things for supper.

"Well," Grandma said, taking her place at the table, "I suppose you've been planning some adventure for

Wednesday." Her smile said she was glad they were there. The children began to eat hungrily.

Lauren said, "I just swam. And then I guess I took a nap on the sand dunes." She tried to sound casual so Tom wouldn't guess she was planning anything.

Tom was glad to bite into his ear of corn. He, too, did not want Lauren to suspect he had his own plans for adventure.

But suddenly Lauren remembered. "Grandma, you said there was another surprise about this week. What is it?"

"It's about your cousin, Elizabeth," Grandma answered. "She's coming tomorrow all the way from Rome, Italy, to pay us a visit."

"Cousin Elizabeth!" Lauren squealed. Her knife clattered to the table.

Tom choked on a mouthful of muffin. "Tomorrow? Why?"

Grandma said calmly, "She's my grandchild, just like you and Lauren are, and I've never seen her."

"Tell us again about Elizabeth," Lauren said. "I've kind of forgotten about her."

"Well, Elizabeth's father was my son, just like your father," Grandma started. "He went to Italy years ago. There he married a beautiful Italian girl, and after a while they had Elizabeth."

"I remember now," Lauren began. "Her parents were killed in a car accident and Elizabeth went to live with an aunt."

16

"That's right," Grandma agreed, "only there are three aunts who have taken care of her."

Tom could hardly control his disappointment. He had thought Grandma had something great in store for them. Now there would be one more girl to get away from. "But why did she decide to come visit you right now?"

"I invited her," Grandma explained. "I thought it would be nice to have her here now so she would have company her own age."

"I'm not going to like her," Tom declared with a scowl.

"Why not?" Lauren asked.

Tom had to think a minute. "Because she'll be fat and smell of garlic."

This wild statement gave Lauren the giggles.

"Well, she will," Tom repeated, " 'cause in Italy they eat spaghetti all the time."

"I seem to remember that you like spaghetti pretty well yourself," Grandma reminded.

"I wonder how they named her Elizabeth," Lauren remarked. "Is that an Italian name?"

"She was named after me," Grandma told her.

Lauren felt a stab of envy. This strange cousin would probably be Grandma's favorite because she was her namesake. Lauren felt resentment mingle with envy. Elizabeth probably wouldn't like owls, and she'd have to get away from her. It wasn't fair. Grandma was the one who was giving them a bitter pill to swallow.

The next day Grandma asked both Tom and Lauren

to stay at the cottage to greet Elizabeth. Mr. Bunby offered to meet the plane, but neither Tom nor Lauren wanted to go with him.

Tom was absolutely sure that he wasn't going to like Elizabeth. He watched with fuming impatience for Mr. Bunby's car to pull up. "I think Elizabeth is a pill," Tom growled to Lauren in the front yard.

"Well, that's what I think, too," Lauren agreed. "Or maybe it's that witch's spoon in the curio cabinet that cast a crazy spell on Grandma."

"That's dopey," Tom snorted. "I don't believe in spells or witches."

A kind of curiosity mingled with Lauren's resentment. Part of her wanted to see Elizabeth. A girl cousin her own age would have been fun if she hadn't made her plans about the baby owls. And there was that heavy, funny feeling of dread that Grandma would love Elizabeth more than she loved them.

"Maybe we can make things so terrible for Elizabeth that she won't want to stay," Tom suggested to Lauren. He kicked at the white picket fence.

Secretly Lauren thought this was going too far, but because she felt so grumpy and mixed up herself, she mumbled, "Maybe we can."

"Pick a nice bunch of sweet peas for the table, dear," Grandma called from the kitchen window.

"O.K.," Lauren replied, and she began to pick flowers.

"How about a horned toad in Elizabeth's bed?" Tom suggested.

"No," Lauren protested. "Grandma will probably want her to sleep next to me, and it might get into my bed. We could knot the sheets in the bed next to mine."

Tom did not reply. He seemed to be thinking.

"Do you know if there are Italian owls?" Lauren asked. Then immediately she wished she hadn't asked. She certainly didn't want Tom to guess her secret adventure.

But Tom was thinking of something else. "Take those old flowers in to Grandma." He spoke so gruffly that Lauren thought she'd better get out of his way. As she started into the cottage, she saw Tom go into the tool shed. What was he going to do there?

In the tool shed Tom looked around for a rope. Lauren's suggestion that they tie knots in the sheets of the bed Elizabeth would sleep in had given him an idea. He found a piece of rope that looked old but seemed strong. Then he carefully tied knots in it about every twelve inches.

This was the rope he would use when he let himself down to the entrance of the forbidden cave. It would be easier if he could reach for a knot. After that he hunted around for a sack. The only one available still held a little garden fertilizer, but he dumped it into a flower pot and put the rope inside the sack. His spirits rose. He knew he was using his head in making such careful preparations. Now all he needed was a flashlight and some food.

At last, when it was afternoon, there was the chug of Mr. Bunby's old car making the climb up the hill. Then everyone was greeting Elizabeth, and Grandma held her so long in a big hug that Lauren was just sure Grandma

was going to love her best. Elizabeth explained the plane had been delayed to make repairs.

Tom had to admit that Elizabeth was certainly not fat. Nor did she smell of garlic. She was very slim, with large dark eyes and shiny long black hair. She wore a white skirt and sweater and her suitcase was shiny black patent leather. It looked foreign.

"Gosh, you speak English," Tom blurted in surprise. Actually she spoke very well, with only a little odd way of pronouncing words.

"Of course." Elizabeth gave him a smile. "In Rome I go to an international school. We are all taught English as well as Italian."

"My dearest child!" Grandma said, wiping a tear from her cheek.

Lauren could hardly bear that. Grandma sometimes called them "dear," but she never said, "My dearest child."

Grandma seemed to be looking and looking at Elizabeth as if she wanted to see something special there. "You do look a little like your father," Grandma said at last.

Why was it grownups were always interested in whether a child looked like a parent? Lauren wondered glumly. Why shouldn't children just look like themselves?

Tom took this opportunity to go to the kitchen to get Grandma's flashlight from the cupboard. He slipped it under his shirt and ran out of the cottage to the tool shed. His fingers pushed the switch of the flashlight. The beam of the light was very faint.

Tom shook the flashlight in frustration. The battery

was going dead. He couldn't go into a cave without a trusty light. Now he'd have to hike into town, which was about two miles away, and buy a battery. He almost groaned out loud.

Inside the cottage Grandma told Lauren to show Elizabeth which bed she'd have on the sleeping porch.

"You take the bed next to mine," Lauren suggested. "Put your clothes in that chest of drawers."

As Elizabeth started to unpack, Grandma joined them. "Well, my dear," she said to Elizabeth, "I see you knit."

"Yes," Elizabeth replied. "One aunt I live with likes me to knit while she reads aloud."

Lauren started to say, "How awful!" but she choked back the impolite words.

"I brought these knitting needles and some yarn, and I would like to make a sweater for you," Elizabeth said to Lauren.

"How lovely," Grandma exclaimed.

"But will you have time?" Lauren asked, thinking that they had only a week.

"These needles are large and the wool is thick and I can knit quite fast. If I do not finish, I can mail it to you."

Lauren began to feel rather ashamed that she'd resented Elizabeth's coming. "That's neat," she said. "But I thought we'd go swimming now."

"I'll put on my swim suit," Elizabeth replied, "and take my knitting bag so I can start your sweater when we sit on the beach."

"That's thoughtful of you," said Grandma. Then she

22

saw something else among Elizabeth's things. "And do you play this flute?"

"Yes, another aunt I live with part time is very musical. I have had flute lessons for two years."

Grandma shook her head wonderingly. "What a strange life you have pleasing your three aunts. But it will be nice to have some music."

"I will be happy to play for you," Elizabeth said.

The girls were almost ready to start for the beach when Lauren thought of another question. "What does your other aunt want you to do?"

"She likes pretty clothes and parties and she always wants me to look nice," Elizabeth said.

It seemed to Lauren that there was no end to the things Elizabeth could do. Jealousy flared again. Here this new cousin could knit, play the flute, and she certainly had no trouble looking nice.

Lauren saw Tom look admiringly as Elizabeth appeared in a cute little white swim suit. He had put on a clean jersey. To Lauren's surprise he asked Grandma, "Is it O.K. if I hike to town? I want to get something at the store."

Grandma replied, "You may if it's right to the store and straight back."

"See you later," Tom yelled. And then he was off.

What was Tom going to buy in town? And what had he been doing in the tool shed? Lauren was sure Tom had some adventure in mind he didn't want her to share.

Elizabeth had discovered the curio cabinet. While she asked Grandma about it, Lauren slipped away to look inside the tool shed. Maybe she'd find out what Tom had been doing in there.

Suddenly she spied something that she had forgotten. It was the cage Mr. Bunby had made for the black-footed ferret. She would put one of the baby owls in the cage, and she would make a little nest for it there.

But she was sure Tom would not understand. And Elizabeth might think her silly to want to have a pet owl. So she would hide the cage in the woods somewhere safe, and every day she would visit it and feed it bread crumbs and bits of apple and pet it. Then when she had to go back home, she would put it back in the nest with its twin.

She took a cautious look out the tool shed door. When she saw no one in the yard, she grabbed the cage and then on second thought she snatched up a sack she saw. She would put the sack over the cage in the woods to hide it.

She made a dash into the woods. As she sped along, she remembered Grandma's words about using their heads in case there was a nip of danger in what they planned to do. Well, she was certainly using her head. Only there really wasn't even a nip of danger in just taking the baby owl for a week.

She found the perfect place to hide the cage, a cozy hollow near three trees. She put the sack over the cage, just in case. It wasn't until she was arranging the sack that she noticed that the sack felt lumpy. She shook it out and blinked in astonishment to see a length of knotted rope. What was it for?

She just couldn't guess. But as she wandered back

24

through the woods, she began to speculate about Tom. He had been in the tool shed. What would he do with a knotted rope?

She was still thinking about it as she brushed against some tall cinnamon ferns. The soft fuzzy stuff that grew along their stems would be just right to line the little nest she planned. So she took her time to gather as much of the fern fuzz as possible. She also gathered some soft grass, some moss, and a few of the mitten-shaped leaves from the sassafras bushes that grew here and there in the woods.

She didn't really want to go beaching with Elizabeth. So she sat on a log and made the nest, and the late afternoon went by very happily.

Back at the cottage Tom was not happy at all. When he returned from town he was furious to find his sack and the knotted rope gone. Who could have taken it? What was he going to do? He had to have a rope to get down to the cave entrance.

He didn't dare ask Lauren about the sack because she'd pester him with questions and she'd follow him the next morning. First of all, in the morning he'd have to go into town again and buy some rope and then go exploring after that.

Just then Lauren came in. She was barefoot and wearing her bathing suit. But her feet were dirty, not sandy, so Tom knew she had not been at the beach. What had she been up to?

Grandma, frosting a cake, said, "You were going to take Elizabeth to the beach."

"I guess I forgot," Lauren mumbled.

Elizabeth said, "That's all right. This afternoon has been very nice here with Grandmother. She told me about June Day, and she showed me all the interesting things in the curio cabinet. And she said I may choose one thing to take back to Rome when I have to go."

Tom and Lauren looked at one another in shock. They weren't even allowed to open the cabinet without permission. And here Elizabeth was going to be given one of the treasures.

Grandma made a curly swirl in the frosting on the cake. "I'm giving Elizabeth a gift from the cabinet now because she lives so far away. You children will have a choice of what you want when you're older."

Lauren sucked in her breath. It wasn't fair. She wanted to shout, "Don't you dare take the little Noah's Ark with all the little animals!"

Tom felt even more outraged. "Don't take the pearl-handled revolver. That's mine," he blurted.

"Why don't you take the witch's spoon?" Lauren coaxed.

"Yes, take the old witch's spoon," Tom urged, thinking it a treasure he would not want.

"It was used only by good witches to stir love potions," Lauren informed Elizabeth, hoping to make it seem more desirable.

"Was it really?" Elizabeth questioned Grandma.

"So the story goes. But it is said to have another strange power, too. In times of terrible trouble you can look into the bowl of the spoon and see the answer to a riddle. Or the face of someone you love."

"Gee, that sounds creepy," Tom said.

Elizabeth's hand trembled as she took the spoon from the cabinet and held it. Her long black hair fell forward, half covering her face as she stared at the spoon.

"What are you looking for?" Tom asked curiously.

"I thought maybe I could see the face of my American father," Elizabeth said softly. "But I do not see anything."

Grandma went to put an arm around Elizabeth. "The spoon is now very old, so it may have lost its magic powers. Or if it ever had any, whatever people used to see in it was what they wanted to see so much that they just thought they saw something."

"In Italy the good witch brings presents to good children on January 6th," Elizabeth told them.

"What do you get if you're not good?" Tom asked teasingly.

"Coal," said Elizabeth. She put the spoon back in the cabinet. "I will think about what I wish to choose later." Then she brought her flute from her suitcase and began to play. Her tune was rather sad at first, and then it sounded happier.

She really can play, Lauren admitted grudgingly.

Grandma came from the kitchen to exclaim in delight.

All Tom could do was wish the evening and night over with so he could get started for town.

When morning came he was wide awake far too early.

The stores in town wouldn't be open. He felt too restless in bed, so he dressed quietly and went outside. There he saw something he had overlooked—Grandma's clothesline. It was strong—well, fairly strong—and Grandma would be so busy with Elizabeth and her flute tooting and stuff that she certainly wouldn't be hanging out clothes.

Hastily he took the clothesline from its hooks on posts. Now he was all set except for a sandwich. In the kitchen he found bread and plum jam. He put the sandwich into the back pocket of his jeans. No time to hunt for a bag for the sandwich or a bottle of pop in the refrigerator. He just wanted to be on his way.

The chalk squeaked on the blackboard as he wrote the single word "beach" after his name. For a moment he thought he heard soft footsteps on the sleeping porch, but no one appeared.

With the coiled clothesline and the flashlight he bounded off.

There was no one on the beach. This was partly because it was early and overnight a stiff north wind had come up, whipping the sea into giant waves that slammed onto the beach. The sky was purple gray, and the sea birds huddled in the little hollows of the rocks for protection.

Tom scrambled up the rocks as quickly as possible, and there he sat knotting the clothesline. Then he tied a loop around the jagged pinnacle and made his way down hand under hand to the cave entrance. Someone, at one time, had blocked the entrance to the cave with a rock. This was

possibly to prevent anyone from going in. But the rock had rolled a bit to one side. There was just room for a limber boy of ten to snake through.

A cold draft of air came out of the cave as he made his way in on hands and knees. He felt chilly and hot and excited all at the same time. His flashlight showed him the way along the tunnel-like path.

Just as he had heard, the tunnel widened to what was almost a room. This was not the room with the queer,

petrified-elephant figures. Tom flashed his light upward
to gaze in wonder at the fascinating crystal formations like
long Christmas-tree icicle decorations that hung from the
top of the cave. Stalactites they were called. Long words
were fun when they were connected with things as exciting
as this. He felt elated to say the word aloud and for the
sheer pleasure of hearing the echo of his voice.

Along with the echo there was a queer rustling sound.
There were bats up there. Well, there were always bats

roosting in caves. He had halfway wished Lauren could see the cave. But even though she was so crazy about animals and birds, he felt certain she would not like bats. And there was the funny story about how bats liked to get in women's and girls' hair. Lauren would certainly feel creepy about that.

He walked on further. The beam of light from his flashlight revealed a stream of water. He got down on his knees to study it. He knew there were blind fish that lived in such black streams. He thought he saw one. Yes, there it was—something like a catfish with whiskers sticking out from its chin.

He put a hand down into the water and just for a second the queer fish remained motionless against it. "Gee," he said aloud, "I could catch this old fish with just my bare hand." It was a rare experience. "I'm king of the cave!" he shouted.

Tom was not as keen about nature lore as Lauren, but now he recalled something about catfish. Either the father or the mother fish picked up the eggs and held them in their mouths until the young hatched. Could this catfish have a mouthful of eggs?

After that two things happened at once. A queer, lizard-like creature darted from a crevice in the rocky wall and startled him. At the same time what seemed like a solid stream of bats coming from every direction descended to swoop around him.

"Hey, I'm not a girl!" he yelled angrily. "You don't need to get in my hair."

He knew it was silly to be yelling at bats. But bats roosting high on the cavern ceiling were one thing and bats circling his head were another. He didn't like it. Still on hands and knees at the stream of water, he struck out against the strange, winged creatures with both hands.

Somehow then, in the mass of swirling bats and his own angry thrashing, he lost his balance. With a sickening lurch he found himself about to fall into the stream of water. Instinctively he grabbed at a rock.

The pounding of his heart shook his body. He had saved himself, but in so doing he had let go of the flashlight. In a daze he heard a splash that was like *plink, plunk, gurgle* as the flashlight went down into the underground river. The circle of light flickered and then went out.

Now he was in pitch dark. He leaned cautiously over the edge of the stream and felt down into the water as far as he could, not minding that his shirt sleeve was soaked. But there was no bottom of the stream to touch.

He sat down on the cave floor, leaning against the rock, weak, angry and frightened. "I mustn't panic," he said aloud. "That's the worst thing I could do."

The echo of his words seemed to bounce against the cave walls and mingle with the sound of the bats' wing beats. He did not feel like king of the cave or an explorer at all any more. He was a lost boy in the pitch dark.

As he started to get up, he felt something wet and gooey drip down his leg. Had he cut himself on a rock? Was it blood?

Feeling down the back of his leg he let out a feeble attempt at a laugh. It was only the jam from his sandwich. In leaning against the rock he had squashed the jam out of his sandwich and it had soaked through his jeans and run down his leg. He was about to throw the sandwich away. But caution told him the bread might be all he'd have to eat for maybe a long time.

Talking aloud made him feel a little braver. "I'll turn around and edge along the river back to the cave opening." Moving on hands and knees, he inched along. Once he touched something hard with crab-like legs that seemed to be inching along, too. And there were scurryings of what he supposed were other small cave animals.

Panic trickled down his spine. "Help!" he yelled. "Help! Help! Help! Don't you hear me? I'm lost." "Lost, lost, lost" came the echo.

"Only the bats hear me," he muttered forlornly. And bats, he knew, didn't need to hear him. They had their own built-in sonar system that made navigation easy and perfect for them in the dark.

"I'll turn around and go back in the other direction," he said. "I've got to keep my cool. Maybe I got mixed up back there." He crept along carefully so as not to fall in the river. He thought he was going in the other direction. Only the stream seemed to flow on and on. He knew it should have gone underground so he would come to the path that led to the cave entrance. Now he was really mixed up.

"But someone will find me," he said, with no feeling

that they would at all. For one thing, he could yell himself hoarse and no one could possibly hear him because of the giant rocks at the cave's entrance.

Then he remembered the wild, stormy weather outside. No one would want to go beaching today. His spirit sank even lower as he recalled that he had written "beach" after his name on Grandma's kitchen blackboard. When people did come to look for him, they'd think he had gone swimming and drowned.

If only he'd thought ahead about the cave being full of bats, he could have brought the beekeeper's hat and veil Grandma wore when she tended her honey bees. For an instant the picture of himself all rigged up in a hat and veil faintly tickled his funny bone, but then he felt more sunk than ever.

Grandma had told them they must think carefully before they opened a box that might hold a bitter pill. Well, the forbidden cave was surely a box with the bitterest pill in the world. Panic really grabbed him now. He couldn't push back the memory of a monster movie he had seen where vampire bats had sucked human blood without the victim feeling it. Of course that was just a movie, he reminded himself, with no courage at all.

The chill of the cave made him shiver. He was hungry, too. His hand went back to his hip pocket to discover that cave beetles had found the jam sandwich a tempting delight. In disgust he tried to shake them off. But he couldn't be sure in the dark, and he didn't want to bite down on a beetle. If only he had tied his flashlight around his neck somehow. If he had his flashlight, he would have enjoyed studying the cave beetles.

Once again he began to inch his way along the edge of the stream. The rough cave floor tore his jeans, and the skin on his knees smarted. But this discomfort was abruptly forgotten as he felt the path take a sharp downward slant. Somewhere he'd made a wrong turn for sure. Maybe it's better if I stick to the cave wall, he thought in confusion. Carefully, he moved sideways, fanning a hand before him in the dark to touch the solid wall.

There it was. But as his hand brushed against the base of the wall, he felt something else that made his stomach draw up tight. Bones! And a skull! He snatched his hand away. He could not see the gruesome find in the dark, and he didn't want to touch the bones again. He didn't want to think that another explorer had lost his way right here and now was just a skeleton.

Or maybe it wasn't another explorer who had lost his way. Maybe long ago one of the pirates, who had buried treasure in the cave room with the rocky elephant-like figures, had hidden out here, waiting for a chance to dig up the treasure and escape with it all for himself. Maybe then he had lost his way and starved to death.

Tom was aware this speculation was pure imagination. But it was less scary to think of a greedy pirate starving to death than an explorer. The pirate might have had some kind of light—maybe matches in a bottle. Or more likely he had had a flint, which Tom knew was a very hard stone you struck against another to make fire.

His hopes of finding this set him on a feverish search. Even touching the bones again didn't make him shudder this time. If he had light for just a minute, he could perhaps get his bearings. The flint could be right among the bones if the pirate had kept it in his pocket.

His fingers brushed against the skull and then sorted through the bones. The bones were small. "Animal bones," he said aloud. The whole elaborate picture he'd dreamed up of a pirate starving to death here made him feel pretty silly. But feeling silly didn't make him any the less lost and desperate. He stood up and took a few cautious steps to ease the cramps in his legs. And that was when he heard the weird sound. A sound like a deep growl. It came again. And again.

He squashed himself against the craggy cave wall. Bears! Bears as well as bats lived in caves. His whole body seemed petrified while the sound continued at regular intervals. The entire cave was filled with the sickening smell of bats, but a bear might have gotten a whiff of his human smell.

The growling sound was so close that it might be coming from a rocky ledge above. He dared not move a muscle for fear of giving away his position. But when nothing attacked him, Tom's fright began to be replaced by curiosity. The bear might be asleep and snoring. Come to think of it, he decided, the sound was more like a long, heavy snore than a growl.

Another puzzling thought followed. How had the bear entered the cave? When he recalled the slim space at the cave entrance where the blocking rock had rolled away, he knew it would not have been possible for a bulky bear to slither through.

Tom took courage to move a few steps away from the sound. As he did so, his sneaker caught on the rocky path and he toppled toward the wall. Catching himself there, he realized that the sound was coming from the other side of the wall, which at this point was made of huge boulders. He put his ear to a chink between the boulders and listened.

It wasn't a bear growl or snore at all. It was the sea he heard—the pounding roar of gigantic waves slamming on rock somewhere out there beyond the cave.

Tom knew how water could gouge out a tunnel. There was just such a tunnel down the beach beyond the rocks that guarded the entrance to the cave. That must be it. Certainly the sea beat its stormy fury against the rocks there. *Boom. Boom. Boom.* The smell of the sea crept through the tiny cracks between the boulders. Oh, how good it was to smell something fresh instead of bats!

But it made him more than ever long for freedom, fresh air, the woods, the cottage, with Grandma cooking in the kitchen. Oh, how he longed to see Grandma and Lauren or even Elizabeth. Was it breakfast time? Were they eating Grandma's yummy pancakes with clover honey and maybe crispy bacon? What was Lauren doing? Did she have some adventure of her own planned for June Day?

Of course Lauren had her own adventure. When she woke, she was very thankful Tom was not in his bed nor in the cottage. Elizabeth and Grandma were still fast asleep. She dressed in haste. Just before she left, she remembered to write her name on the kitchen blackboard. She didn't want to say she was going to the owl tree. That would be a sure giveaway, so she wrote "beach." After all, she would be halfway to the beach. For just the tiniest minute she wondered what Tom was doing at the beach so early because there was his name with "beach" after it.

Outside, a blast of the north wind whipped her bright hair straight back from her face. He legs moved with record speed on the way past Mr. Bunby's house and then to the edge of the bluff. She saw the purple, storm-tossed waves of the ocean, but she felt glowing inside with excitement. In just a few minutes now she would be holding the baby owl.

As she scampered down to the owl tree, she was glad it was such a bad day. No one would come upon her climbing to the owl's nest. Soon I'll be taking my baby owl to the cage hidden in the pine trees, and he'll be mine for a whole week, she thought happily.

The only trouble was that climbing the owl tree was not the easy task she had thought. Though she had grown some this year, the foothold branches were still too far apart. She tried again and again, stretching every muscle.

Lauren stood on the bench looking up. There they were —the two tiny heads looking at her, so near yet so out of reach. But she wasn't giving up. Not with the cage and the little nest waiting.

"I'll get Mr. Bunby's ladder," she decided aloud. "The small one I can carry." With a renewed spurt of energy she flew up the steps and back to Mr. Bunby's yard on the side where his pear trees grew.

The small ladder was just right. She managed it very nicely, dragging it, then bumping it down the stairs to the owl tree. Getting the ladder up on the bench was harder. She was puffing and perspiring, in spite of the nippy wind, by the time she had the ladder resting on the bench against the owl tree.

She climbed the ladder slowly, not looking down. The ladder was a little bit tippy, and if she fell she would have a terrible tumble down the bluff into all the brambles below.

At the last rung of the ladder it was still a long stretch to the nest. Her fingers touched the opening in the tree and then a tiny owl head. Oh, it was the softest thing she'd ever felt. She was beside herself with delight.

Lauren had pictured herself selecting which owl she would take. It would be the one with the wisest look in his big eyes, the most appealing and the most cuddly looking.

Only out of nowhere, it seemed, with no sound of warning wings, a heavy object landed on her head, almost toppling her from her perch. Powerful claws dug into her scalp. A huge, hooked bill pecked her forehead. She had not counted on the mother owl coming back to her little ones while she was on the ladder.

"Go away! Go away!" she screamed in fright. Clasping the tree with both arms to keep from losing balance and falling, she tried to shake the mother owl loose from her head. But it was no use. The mother owl was fiercely angry.

In a daze of terror she heard the little owlets make a kind of whistling sound as they watched from their nest.

Lauren kept her eyes tightly shut against the cruel pecks ofthe mother owl's bill. "Help! Help!" she shrieked. With the big owl clasped to her head, she dared not try to go back down the ladder, and she dared not let go of the tree for fear of falling. "Tom, Tom!" she screamed into the wind. "Tom, Tom, Tom!"

In the midst of her terror she remembered Grandma's words about finding a bitter pill in a box of adventure she might open. She had certainly found hers. But what was she going to do?

Then she was startled to hear Elizabeth's voice below the ladder. "Do as I tell you, Lauren," she called with such firm authority that Lauren stopped her yelling. "Keep your eyes closed. Hold onto the tree," Elizabeth commanded. "Now take one step down the ladder."

Lauren obeyed. But the mother owl remained clamped on her head.

"I'm coming up to you," Elizabeth said. "Hold on. I'm almost up to you."

Lauren felt the ladder quiver a bit under Elizabeth's weight.

"Now put your right hand down," Elizabeth told her. "Here is one of my knitting needles. Wave it round and round over your head."

Lauren did as she was instructed. After a few waves the big mother owl flew off her head, and both girls scrambled down the ladder.

"Whatever were you doing up there?" Elizabeth asked.

With a sob Lauren dropped down on the bench in tears of disappointment and relief. "I just wanted to borrow one of the baby owls for a week," she choked. She went on to explain about the cage waiting in the woods, how it had been her heart's desire to hold and pet a baby owl.

To Lauren's great surprise, Elizabeth understood. "I

hid a kitten in the attic once," Elizabeth confided. "My aunts don't like cats. The kitten was discovered and given away. I'll never forget how heartbroken I was."

Lauren swiped at her tear-stained face. "Grandma told us if there was even a nip of danger in what we wanted to do on our June Day we must think carefully. I—I guess I didn't think carefully enough because I got nipped."

Elizabeth found a tissue in her knitting bag and wiped some tiny blood spots from Lauren's forehead, and she helped Lauren brush bits of bark from the front of her sweater. "Lucky I saw your name on the blackboard with 'beach' written after it, and Grandmother pointed out the way."

"And lucky you brought your knitting bag and could give me a knitting needle," Lauren added. "I must have looked funny with that big old bird on my head," she said, trying to ease her disappointment.

Elizabeth nodded and both girls went into giggles for a minute. "I'll help you carry the ladder up the stairs," she offered.

At the cottage there was the good smell of pancakes and bacon frying. Lauren scampered into the bathroom to wash her face and comb her bangs down over her owl-pecked forehead.

"There's a mystery here," Grandma announced. "My clothesline has disappeared, and there was a large blob of jam spilled on the kitchen floor."

"Who would take your clothesline?" Lauren asked. But

then she remembered the knotted rope in the bag she found in the tool shed. Tom must have wanted a rope for something. She wondered what he had in mind.

The morning passed with no answer to the puzzling question. Because it was such a windy day, the girls spent their time indoors playing games from Grandma's game cupboard, and more and more Lauren found it was fun to have a girl cousin like Elizabeth.

But there was one more puzzling thing. Elizabeth was good at games, but she seemed to be thinking of something else a lot of the time—something that made her look worried.

At noon they had lunch without Tom. "I wonder what adventure Tom is finding on such a day?" Grandma remarked, sounding as worried as Elizabeth. "I do hope he's not being reckless."

Yes, what could he be doing? Lauren asked herself. The blackboard said he was at the beach, but no one would want to spend a whole day there in this howling wind, and no one could go swimming in such wild waves.

Time and again Grandma went out to the road to look one way and then the other, shaking her head in anxiety.

About four o'clock, when the girls were tired of playing games, Elizabeth said to Lauren, "Let's take a walk." So the girls went out. Almost at once Elizabeth began to talk about what was worrying her.

"It's the witch's spoon," she confided. "First thing this morning I looked at it again. When I looked at it last night and Grandmother said maybe I could see the face of someone I loved in it, I hoped to see my father's face." Her voice trembled a bit. "I do not remember my father, and I long to see him."

"You don't really believe in such magic," Lauren half scoffed.

"Last night I saw nothing in the spoon at all," Elizabeth went on. "But this morning I saw Tom's face."

"You did? You really saw Tom?"

Elizabeth's long dark hair swayed as her head nodded. "I'm sure."

By now the girls had reached the beach. The wind tore at them, and the roar of the ocean almost drowned their voices.

"We must search for Tom," Elizabeth said firmly.

Though Lauren still could not quite believe in the power of the witch's spoon, she was caught up in Elizabeth's obvious anxiety. "We'll look around the sand dunes. He might be there."

But Tom was not to be found among the sand dunes nor was he on the deserted shore. The girls shouted his name over and over.

They came to the castle-like barrier of rocks. Elizabeth asked, "Could Tom be on the other side of these great rocks?"

A sinking sensation came to Lauren's stomach. In a dreadful flash of understanding Tom's need for a rope, she guessed where he was. Lauren huddled against the

48

rocks to get out of the wind and drew Elizabeth to her. "There's a hidden cave beyond the rocks. We've never been in because it's dangerous to explore. Most people don't even know the entrance is here."

"You think Tom might be there?" Elizabeth asked, wide-eyed.

Both girls scrambled up the rocks, slipping and sliding on the slick surfaces. At the pinnacle, where the clothesline was tied, they paused for breath. Now they knew for certain.

"Tom, Tom!" both girls screamed. The wind blew their screams away.

"He'll never hear us," Lauren said at last, "and we dare not go in the cave or *we'll* get lost."

Elizabeth was already letting herself down the rope hand under hand. Lauren followed. They crouched at the mouth of the cave and shouted till they were all shouted out. "I think we must tell Grandmother and get a rescue party," Elizabeth said at last.

"If Tom is really in trouble, we will never be allowed to come visit Grandma again," Lauren wailed. "That's what she warned us. She told us we must use our heads." Not quite believing what she said she added, "Maybe Tom isn't really lost in the cave. Maybe he'll just walk out."

Elizabeth shook her head. "It's almost dark. And I have this feeling Tom is in trouble." She put her hands over her face and rocked back and forth in thought. "In

49

Italy there are many caves. I have been in one with a guide. We all held a rope that kept us together." Elizabeth's voice ran down. "I have an idea," she said. "You wait here. I must go back to the cottage and get something."

Before Lauren could ask what her idea was, Elizabeth was gone. It seemed hours to Lauren, crouched at the narrow opening to the cave, until Elizabeth returned. Actually it was only about twenty minutes. To her astonishment Elizabeth had her knitting and her flute. She held up the ball of yarn. "This yarn is heavy and strong. I'm going to tie one end around me. You hold the other. You must let it out bit by bit while I go into the cave and play my flute. Some musical notes can be heard far beyond the sound of a voice. Maybe Tom will hear."

"You're going in in the dark?" Lauren gasped.

"No, I remembered this candle in Grandmother's cupboard. I've brought matches and will light it when I'm in the cave. I know there are side paths where one might get lost in a cave. But perhaps—just perhaps—Tom will hear me and that will help him find his way."

Lauren could only stare dumbfounded. "It might be scary in there."

Elizabeth said, "This yarn will help me return safely." But her voice was not too sure.

"I'll let out the yarn very carefully," Lauren assured her. She watched as Elizabeth put the flute in her knitting bag and tied the drawstring around her waist. She looped the yarn through her belt and put the knitting in her

slacks pocket. In another moment she was down on hands and knees.

"Oh, do be careful," Lauren warned. On impulse she threw her arms around Elizabeth and gave her a squeeze.

Inside the cave, Tom had lost his last bit of courage. Even if rescuers did find him before he starved to death he knew he was in the worst trouble of his whole life. He would never be allowed to come to visit Grandma again. That's what Grandma had told them when she warned them that she was trusting them to use judgment.

Hunger drove him to eat the jam sandwich. He just gulped it down, trying not to notice if he crunched on a crisp beetle. Then he dipped into the stream for a drink of water. He thought he touched the catfish again.

Every story he had read of people lost in desperate places came to his mind. He knew some people avoided starvation by catching and eating whatever small animals they could. But even if he could really catch the catfish, he was sure he would never be able to bite into it raw. And if he was able to grab a cave lizard, he was equally sure he could not eat it raw, either. And besides if you grabbed a lizard or salamander by the tail, it was said the tail simply pulled off and the animals grew a new one.

He shuddered at the gruesome thought. He would rather starve. He wished he could leave a message for Grandma and Lauren. Out of some back pocket of his mind he re-called reading about a cave dweller who had written notes on a dried bat wing. He knew he was surrounded by thousands of bats overhead, and there certainly must be dried bat wings somewhere, but he couldn't find them in the dark. And he had no pencil.

Once he and some other boys had pretended to write pirate notes in blood, using mulberry juice for blood. Now he wished he hadn't eaten that plum jam sandwich. Maybe he could at least have written "goodbye" with a finger and plum jam on the cave wall.

He sat down and leaned against the cold wall. He tried hard not to mind the smell of bats, but it was pretty overwhelming. Worn out by fright, his head nodded to one side, and he began to dream a scary dream about a snake trying to twine around his arm. In the dark he couldn't see the color of the snake, but his dream thought went over that warning he'd learned in nature class at school:

> Red and yellow
> Kill a fellow.

Was the snake red and yellow? He struggled to get away from the snake and the dream. And then he was awake. The snake had been his wet shirt sleeve. And he really wasn't sure he was wide awake. In the blackness of the cave he thought maybe he was dead and he was hearing strange, heavenly music.

He pinched himself. "Ouch!" No, he wasn't dead.

Tom strained to hear where the music was coming from. Daring no more than a step at a time so he wouldn't fall into the stream, he felt his way toward what he thought

53

was someone signaling to him. His heart lifted. Surely that was it. A signal. He had not cried before, but now he had to blink back tears of relief.

As the sound grew louder, he knew what the music was. It was Elizabeth's flute. Elizabeth, whom he had resented and disliked, had come to his rescue.

A feeble ray of light showed him that he had made a turn from the main path. Then, the turn made, he was in the first cavern room. There was Elizabeth playing her flute. A candle set in the dirt at her feet gave a wavering light—the most welcome bit of light in the whole world.

"Elizabeth!" The name rocketed and then echoed through the cavern, and Elizabeth met him with happy tears streaming down her face.

"Gosh, Elizabeth—oh, golly am I glad to see you! Am I ever glad!" He started to tell her how he had lost his flashlight. But suddenly he was so choked up with thankfulness that he could not get another word out.

When Lauren saw Tom crawl out of the cave with Elizabeth, she, too, wanted to cry with relief. But she knew Tom wouldn't like that. So she gulped, "Are you a mess! You've even lost one of your sneakers."

Elizabeth said, "Grandmother has been terribly worried about you because of the stormy weather."

"But this is our June Day when we're allowed to do anything we want," Tom reminded.

Running back along the beach, they hatched a plan. The girls would talk to Grandma in the front of the cottage while Tom slipped in the back way and changed his

muddy clothes as fast as he could.

Their plan worked.

Grandma and chicken and dumplings ready for supper all looked so good to Tom that he could hardly bear it.

They all sat down at the table and Grandma said, "I'm sorry you didn't have sunshine on your June Day, but I hope you had some adventures anyway."

For a tiny minute Lauren relived the bitter pill of disappointment she had to swallow about the baby owl. She pushed her fork into a chicken dumpling. "I had a real adventure," she said. "This morning a great big owl came and sat right on my head."

Grandma shook her head in astonishment, and her eyes twinkled. "My, my," she said in that tone that grownups use when they don't really believe what children are saying, "that was an adventure!"

She passed Tom the dish of cranberry sauce. "You must have had an even more exciting adventure, since you were gone all day."

Tom lowered his head so he would not meet Grandma's glance. "Yeah, I sure did." Then, the words tumbling out, he said, "I caught a big old catfish with my bare hands, or I could have caught it. I let it swim away."

"Just think of that!" Grandma remarked. "Not many boys would miss a chance to catch a fish with their bare hands."

Tom realized this sounded pretty dumb so he added, "I was going to write you a letter on a dried bat wing only

I couldn't find a dried bat wing." This story sounded even dumber so he said, "Anyway, I didn't have a pencil."

Grandma really laughed out loud. She said, "I know one thing. I have just about the most imaginative grandchildren in the world.

Both Tom and Lauren gulped. If Grandma only knew. But they didn't dare tell.

"By the way," Grandma said, "my clothesline disappeared mysteriously today."

Tom managed an impish grin. "Well, it's been mysteriously returned now."

The children looked at one another. Was Grandma going to question Tom further?

But Grandma turned to Elizabeth. "And what did you do today? I know you weren't out long, but did you have any skirmishes with owls or catfishes or bats?"

Evading the question, Elizabeth replied "I thought about what I want from the curio cabinet." She left her place at the table and went to the cabinet and took out the witch's spoon. Standing there, she noticed something she had not paid attention to before. On the wall beside the cabinet there were framed pictures of both Lauren and Tom. She took the spoon in her hands. Had the light been just right to reflect Tom's image from the picture to the polished bowl of the spoon? No, she wanted to think of it as a magic spoon that could do magic things. In a way it had done magic things. Tom and Lauren were now her friends. "I'm certain that I want the witch's spoon," she told Grandma.

"Gee, you could have the pearl-handled pistol," Tom urged in a burst of generosity.

"Or the little Noah's Ark with all the animals," Lauren offered eagerly.

"But I want the witch's spoon," Elizabeth repeated. "Grandmother," she asked, "may I stir the tea with it?"

Grandma took the lid from the teapot set next to her plate. It was what Grandma called "Summer Mist Tea," made from sage, linden flowers and strawberry leaves. Elizabeth gave the tea three stirs.

Grandma said, "Now you must all remember the witch's spoon has magic power. When we drink this tea—"

"It will be a real love potion," Lauren finished for her.

Tom was about to snort, "Mush and slush," but he remembered Elizabeth standing in the cave in the flickering candlelight. The sound of her flute was still loud and clear in his ears. She was clever and brave, as well as being the prettiest girl he had ever seen. If she wanted to think of the old spoon as a witch's spoon he guessed that was O.K.

Grandma poured the tea. They all drank.

Suddenly Lauren jumped up and down, wild with excitement. "I just had an idea, Elizabeth! Why don't you come home with us at the end of the week and stay as long as your aunts will let you? You can share my room. Oh, we could have fun."

"Yeah, that would be neat," Tom chimed in.

Grandma looked at Lauren's and Tom's eager faces, and the bright happiness in Elizabeth's dark eyes. "Well,

I declare," she said, her voice a bit unsteady, "the witch's spoon hasn't lost its powers at all." She lifted the teapot. "This is a true love potion, and I'm going to have a second cup."

MARY CUNNINGHAM now lives
in Hollywood, California. Before she started a career in
writing, she taught in a private
school for exceptional children,
and she also worked with children in an Italian settlement
house. Since then, she has pub-
lished short stories, written for
radio, and been a successful
playwright. *Secret of the Sea
Witch* was her first book for
younger readers. Other books
for young people include
*The Paris Hat, Mystery at
Clover House,* and *The
Missing Emerald.*